The Five Orange Pips

THE ADVENTURES OF SHERLOCK HOLMES

SIR ARTHUR CONAN DOYLE

TWAGAA
HTTPS://TWAGAA.COM

Published by

TWAGAA

HTTPS://TWAGAA.COM

TWAGAA INTERNATIONAL
Mumbai (Maharashtra), India
Email: hello@twagaa.com
Website: https://twagaa.com

Illustrations by Sidney Edward Paget
Illustrations sourced from 'Victorian Web' < http://www.victorianweb.org/ > and 'The Arthur Conan Doyle Encyclopedia <https://www.arthur-conan-doyle.com/>
Illustrations re-mastered by Seek Red <https://seekred.com/>
Book & cover design by Sucharita Suri <https://sucharitas.world/>

Title: The Five Orange Pips - The Adventures of Sherlock Holmes
ISBN ebook: 978-93-95164-63-4
ISBN Paperback: 978-93-95164-91-7

First Edition
Published in India

10 9 8 7 6 5 4 3 2 1

The Five Orange Pips

THE ADVENTURES OF SHERLOCK HOLMES

What's Inside

Welcome, Mr. Holmes!

Dear Readers,

Step into a world of enigma, deduction, and the unparalleled genius of Sherlock Holmes with "The Five Orange Pips," an enthralling tale from Arthur Conan Doyle's timeless collection, "The Adventures of Sherlock Holmes." Brace yourself for a whirlwind of mystery as Holmes and his steadfast comrade, Dr. John Watson, navigate the convoluted path of a sinister puzzle that will keep you perched on the edge of your seat.

Within the pages of this book, we extend to you an invitation that goes beyond the mere enjoyment of the riveting narrative. Embark on an interactive journey that combines exploration and imagination, as we delve into the heart of "The Five Orange Pips." This isn't merely a story; it's an opportunity to glean insights that transcend the plot and resonate in your own life.

Challenge your intellect with an engaging quiz designed to probe the depths of the characters, motives, and intricacies woven into the tale. Embark on a cerebral adventure with a skillfully crafted crossword puzzle, featuring prominent figures from the narrative. Take a moment to vividly visualize the unfolding scenes through guided visualization exercises. And don't hesitate to unleash your creativity through captivating writing prompts, inviting you to weave your own detective narrative inspired by the brilliant Holmes.

Whether you're an ardent aficionado of Holmes' astute deductions or a newcomer lured by the enigma of mystery, this book promises an expedition like no other. "The Five Orange Pips" is more than a story; it's an invitation to explore, to learn, and to create in the company of one of literature's most iconic personalities.

Celebrate the timeless legacy of Sherlock Holmes and the captivating realm of Arthur Conan Doyle. Here's to embracing your inner Holmes!

Enjoy your reading and let your creativity flow!

Editor

A quick intro to the story

THE FIVE ORANGE PIPS

"The Five Orange Pips" is a captivating narrative from "The Adventures of Sherlock Holmes" by Arthur Conan Doyle. In this tale, Sherlock Holmes, the astute detective, is confronted with a perplexing case brought forth by John Openshaw. Openshaw seeks Holmes' aid in deciphering a series of mysterious and ominous letters. These letters, each containing five dried orange pips, have caused the death of his uncle and his father in apparent accidents. Openshaw is now the target of the same sinister correspondence and fears for his life.

Holmes delves into the enigma with his characteristic brilliance, employing his keen observational skills to unravel the intricate details. As he pieces together the evidence, Holmes discerns a dark history behind the letters—a history intertwined with a secret society seeking vengeance. Through his meticulous investigation, Holmes uncovers the origins of the pips and exposes the grim intent behind them.

Despite Holmes' best efforts to protect Openshaw, tragedy strikes once more, leaving Holmes with a palpable sense of frustration and the unsettling realization that some mysteries remain unsolvable. The narrative not only showcases Holmes' unmatched deductive prowess but also introduces the theme of unresolved terror, accentuated by the recurring motif of the orange pips.

"The Five Orange Pips" not only offers a tantalizing puzzle but also provides a glimpse into Holmes' unwavering commitment to justice and his ability to confront the unexplainable. As the tale unfolds, readers are drawn into the intricate web of fear and intrigue, experiencing firsthand the relentless pursuit of truth that defines the legendary detective's character.

THE STORY?

When I glance over my notes and records of the Sherlock Holmes cases between the years '82 and '90, I am faced by so many which present strange and interesting features that it is no easy matter to know which to choose and which to leave. Some, however, have already gained publicity through the papers, and others have not offered a field for those peculiar qualities which my friend possessed in so high a degree, and which it is the object of these papers to illustrate. Some, too, have baffled his analytical skill, and would be, as narratives, beginnings without an ending, while others have been but partially cleared up, and have their explanations founded rather upon conjecture and surmise than on that absolute logical proof which was so dear to him. There is, however, one of these last which was so remarkable in its details and so startling in its results that I am tempted to give some account of it in spite of the fact that there are points in connection with it which never have been, and probably never will be, entirely cleared up.

The year '87 furnished us with a long series of cases of greater or less interest, of which I retain the records. Among my headings under this one twelve months I find an account of the adventure of the Paradol Chamber, of the Amateur Mendicant Society, who held a luxurious club in the lower vault of a furniture warehouse, of the facts connected with the loss of the British barque Sophy Anderson, of the singular adventures of the Grice Patersons in the island of Uffa, and finally of the Camberwell poisoning case. In the latter, as may be remembered, Sherlock Holmes was able, by winding up the dead man's watch, to prove that it had been wound up two hours before, and that therefore the deceased had gone to bed within that time—a deduction which was of the greatest importance in clearing up the case. All these I may sketch out at some future date, but none of them present such singular features as the strange train of circumstances which I have now taken up my pen to describe.

It was in the latter days of September, and the equinoctial gales had set in with exceptional violence. All day the wind had screamed and the rain had beaten against the windows, so that even here in the heart of great, hand-made London we were forced to raise our minds for the instant from the routine of life and to recognise the presence of those great elemental forces which shriek at mankind through the bars of his civilisation, like untamed beasts in a cage. As evening drew in, the storm grew higher and louder, and the wind cried and sobbed like a child in the chimney. Sherlock Holmes sat moodily at one side of the fireplace cross-indexing his records of crime, while I at the other was deep in one of Clark Russell's fine sea-stories until the howl of the gale from without seemed to blend with the text, and the splash of the rain to lengthen out into the long swash of the sea waves. My wife was on a visit to her mother's, and for a few days I was a dweller once more in my old quarters at Baker Street.

"Why", said I, glancing up at my companion, "that was surely the bell. Who could come to-night? Some friend of yours, perhaps?"

"Except yourself I have none", he answered. "I do not encourage visitors".

"A client, then?"

"If so, it is a serious case. Nothing less would bring a man out on such a day and at such an hour. But I take it that it is more likely to be some crony of the landlady's".

Sherlock Holmes was wrong in his conjecture, however, for there came a step in the passage and a tapping at the door. He stretched out his long arm to turn the lamp away from himself and towards the vacant chair upon which a newcomer must sit.

"Come in!" said he.

The man who entered was young, some two-and-twenty at the outside, well-groomed and trimly clad, with something of refinement and delicacy in his bearing. The streaming umbrella which he held in his hand, and his long shining waterproof told of the fierce weather through which he had come. He looked about him anxiously in the glare of the lamp, and I could see that his face was pale and his eyes heavy, like those of a man who is weighed down with some great anxiety.

He looked about him anxiously

"I owe you an apology", he said, raising his golden pince-nez to his eyes. "I trust that I am not intruding. I fear that I have brought some traces of the storm and rain into your snug chamber".

"Give me your coat and umbrella", said Holmes. "They may rest here on the hook and will be dry presently. You have come up from the south-west, I see".

"Yes, from Horsham".

"That clay and chalk mixture which I see upon your toe caps is quite distinctive".

"I have come for advice".

"That is easily got".

"And help".

"That is not always so easy".

"I have heard of you, Mr. Holmes. I heard from Major Prendergast how you saved him in the Tankerville Club scandal".

"Ah, of course. He was wrongfully accused of cheating at cards".

"He said that you could solve anything".

"He said too much".

"That you are never beaten".

"I have been beaten four times—three times by men,

and once by a woman".

"But what is that compared with the number of your successes?"

"It is true that I have been generally successful".

"Then you may be so with me".

"I beg that you will draw your chair up to the fire and favour me with some details as to your case".

"It is no ordinary one".

"None of those which come to me are. I am the last court of appeal".

"And yet I question, sir, whether, in all your experience, you have ever listened to a more mysterious and inexplicable chain of events than those which have happened in my own family".

"You fill me with interest", said Holmes. "Pray give us the essential facts from the commencement, and I can afterwards question you as to those details which seem to me to be most important".

The young man pulled his chair up and pushed his wet feet out towards the blaze.

"My name", said he, "is John Openshaw, but my own affairs have, as far as I can understand, little to do with this awful business. It is a hereditary matter; so in order to give you an idea of the facts, I must go back to the commencement of the affair.

"You must know that my grandfather had two sons—my uncle Elias and my father Joseph. My father had a small factory at Coventry, which he enlarged at the time of the invention of bicycling. He was a patentee of the Openshaw unbreakable tire, and his business met with such success that he was able to sell it and to retire upon a handsome competence.

"My uncle Elias emigrated to America when he was a young man and became a planter in Florida, where he was reported to have done very well. At the time of the war he fought in Jackson's army, and afterwards under Hood, where he rose to be a colonel. When Lee laid down his arms my uncle returned to his plantation, where he remained for three or four years. About 1869 or 1870 he came back to Europe and took a small estate in Sussex, near Horsham. He had made a very considerable fortune in the States, and his reason for leaving them was his aversion to the negroes, and his dislike of the Republican policy in extending the franchise to them. He was a singular man, fierce and quick-tempered, very foul-mouthed when he was angry, and of a most retiring disposition. During all the years that he lived at Horsham, I doubt if ever he set foot in the town. He had a garden and two or three fields round his house, and there he would take his exercise, though very often for weeks on end he would never leave his room. He drank a great deal of brandy and smoked very heavily, but he would see no society and did not want any friends, not even his own brother.

"He didn't mind me; in fact, he took a fancy to me, for at the time when he saw me first I was a youngster of twelve or so. This would be in the year 1878, after he had been eight or nine years in England. He begged my father to let me live with him and he was very kind to me in his way. When he was sober he used to be fond of playing backgammon and draughts with me, and he would make me his representative both with the servants and with the tradespeople, so that by the time that I was sixteen I was quite master of the house. I kept all the keys and could go where I liked and do what I liked, so long as I did not disturb him in his privacy. There was one singular exception, however, for he had a single room, a lumber-room up among the attics, which was invariably locked, and which he would never permit either me or anyone else to enter. With a boy's curiosity I have peeped through the keyhole, but I was never able to see more than such a collection of old trunks and bundles as would be expected in such a room.

"One day—it was in March, 1883—a letter with a foreign stamp lay upon the table in front of the colonel's plate. It was not a common thing for him to receive letters, for his bills were all paid in ready money, and he had no friends of any sort. 'From India!' said he as he took it up, 'Pondicherry postmark! What can this be?' Opening it hurriedly, out there jumped five little dried orange pips, which pattered down upon his plate. I began to laugh at this, but the laugh was struck from my lips at the sight of his face. His lip had fallen, his eyes were protruding, his skin the colour of putty, and he glared at the envelope which he still held in his trembling hand, 'K. K. K.!' he shrieked, and then, 'My God, my God, my sins have overtaken me!'

"'What is it, uncle?' I cried.

"'Death,' said he, and rising from the table he retired to his room, leaving me palpitating with horror. I took up the envelope and saw scrawled in red ink upon the inner flap, just above the gum, the letter K three times repeated. There was nothing else save the five dried pips. What could be the reason of his overpowering terror? I left the breakfast-table, and as I ascended the stair I met him coming down with an old rusty key, which must have belonged to the attic, in one hand, and a small brass box, like a cashbox, in the other.

"'They may do what they like, but I'll checkmate them still,' said he with an oath. 'Tell Mary that I shall want a fire in my room today, and send down to Fordham, the Horsham lawyer.'

"I did as he ordered, and when the lawyer arrived I was asked to step up to the room. The fire was burning brightly, and in the grate there was a mass of black, fluffy ashes, as of burned paper, while the brass box stood open and empty beside it. As I glanced at the box I noticed, with a start, that upon the lid was printed the treble K which I had read in the morning upon the envelope.

"'I wish you, John,' said my uncle, 'to witness my will. I leave my estate, with all its advantages and all its disadvantages, to my brother, your father, whence it will, no doubt, descend to you. If you can enjoy it in peace, well and good! If you find you cannot, take my advice, my boy, and leave it to your deadliest enemy. I am sorry to give you such a two-edged thing, but I can't say what turn things are going to take. Kindly sign the paper where Mr. Fordham shows you.'

"I signed the paper as directed, and the lawyer took it away with him. The singular incident made, as you may think, the deepest impression upon me, and I pondered over it and turned it every way in my mind without being able to make anything of it. Yet I could not shake off the vague feeling of dread which it left behind, though the sensation grew less keen as the weeks passed and nothing happened to disturb the usual routine of our lives. I could see a change in my uncle, however. He drank more than ever, and he was less inclined for any sort of society. Most of his time he would spend in his room, with the door locked upon the inside, but sometimes he would emerge in a sort of drunken frenzy and would burst out of the house and tear about the garden with a revolver in his hand, screaming out that he was afraid of no man, and that he was not to be cooped up, like a sheep in a pen, by man or devil. When these hot fits were over, however, he would rush tumultuously in at the door and lock and bar it behind him, like a man who can brazen it out no longer against the terror which lies at the roots of his soul. At such times I have seen his face, even on a cold day, glisten with moisture, as though it were new raised from a basin.

"Well, to come to an end of the matter, Mr. Holmes, and not to abuse your patience, there came a night when he made one of those drunken sallies from which he never came back. We found him, when we went to search for him, face downward in a little green-scummed pool, which lay at the foot of the garden. There was no sign of any violence, and the water was but two feet deep, so that the jury, having regard to his known eccentricity, brought in a verdict of 'suicide.' But I, who knew how he winced from the very thought of death, had much ado to persuade myself that he had gone out of his way to meet it. The matter passed, however, and my father entered into possession of the estate, and of some £14,000, which lay to his credit at the bank".

"One moment", Holmes interposed, "your statement is, I

We found him face downward in a little green scummed pool

foresee, one of the most remarkable to which I have ever listened. Let me have the date of the reception by your uncle of the letter, and the date of his supposed suicide".

"The letter arrived on March 10, 1883. His death was seven weeks later, upon the night of May 2nd".

"Thank you. Pray proceed".

"When my father took over the Horsham property, he, at my request, made a careful examination of the attic, which had been always locked up. We found the brass box there, although its contents had been destroyed. On the inside of the cover was a paper label, with the initials of K. K. K. repeated upon it, and 'Letters, memoranda, receipts, and a register' written beneath. These, we presume, indicated the nature of the papers which had been destroyed by Colonel Openshaw. For the rest, there was nothing of much importance in the attic save a great many scattered papers and note-books bearing upon my uncle's life in America. Some of them were of the war time and showed that he had done his duty well and had borne the repute of a brave soldier. Others were of a date during the reconstruction of the Southern states, and were mostly concerned with politics, for he had evidently taken a strong part in opposing the carpet-bag politicians who had been sent down from the North.

"Well, it was the beginning of '84 when my father came to live at Horsham, and all went as well as possible with us until the January of '85. On the fourth day after the new year I heard my father give a sharp cry of surprise as we sat together at the breakfast-table. There he was, sitting with a newly opened envelope in one hand and five dried orange pips in the outstretched palm of the

What does this mean?

other one. He had always laughed at what he called my cock-and-bull story about the colonel, but he looked very scared and puzzled now that the same thing had come upon himself.

"'Why, what on earth does this mean, John?' he stammered.

"My heart had turned to lead. 'It is K. K. K.,' said I.

"He looked inside the envelope. 'So it is,' he cried. 'Here are the very letters. But what is this written above them?'

"'Put the papers on the sundial,' I read, peeping over his shoulder.

"'What papers? What sundial?' he asked.

"'The sundial in the garden. There is no other,' said I; 'but the papers must be those that are destroyed.'

"'Pooh!' said he, gripping hard at his courage. 'We are in a civilised land here, and we can't have tomfoolery of this kind. Where does the thing come from?'

"'From Dundee,' I answered, glancing at the postmark.

"'Some preposterous practical joke,' said he. 'What have I to do with sundials and papers? I shall take no notice of such nonsense.'

"'I should certainly speak to the police,' I said.

"'And be laughed at for my pains. Nothing of the sort.'

"'Then let me do so?'

"'No, I forbid you. I won't have a fuss made about such nonsense.'

"It was in vain to argue with him, for he was a very obstinate man. I went about, however, with a heart which was full of forebodings.

"On the third day after the coming of the letter my father went from home to visit an old friend of his, Major Freebody, who is in command of one of the forts upon Portsdown Hill. I was glad that he should go, for it seemed to me that he was farther from danger when he was away from home. In that, however, I was in error. Upon the second day of his absence I received a telegram from the major, imploring me to come at once. My father had fallen over one of the deep chalk-pits which abound in the neighbourhood, and was lying senseless, with a shattered skull. I hurried to him, but he passed away without having ever recovered his consciousness. He had, as it appears, been returning from Fareham in the twilight, and as the country was unknown to him, and the chalk-pit unfenced, the jury had no hesitation in bringing in a verdict of 'death from accidental causes.' Carefully as I examined every fact connected with his death, I was unable to find anything which could suggest the idea of murder. There were no signs of violence, no

Shook out five little dried orange pips

footmarks, no robbery, no record of strangers having been seen upon the roads. And yet I need not tell you that my mind was far from at ease, and that I was well-nigh certain that some foul plot had been woven round him.

"In this sinister way I came into my inheritance. You will ask me why I did not dispose of it? I answer, because I was well convinced that our troubles were in some way dependent upon an incident in my uncle's life, and that the danger would be as pressing in one house as in another.

"It was in January, '85, that my poor father met his end, and two years and eight months have elapsed since then. During that time I have lived happily at Horsham, and I had begun to hope that this curse had passed away from the family, and that it had ended with the last generation. I had begun to take comfort too soon, however; yesterday morning the blow fell in the very shape in which it had come upon my father".

The young man took from his waistcoat a crumpled envelope, and turning to the table he shook out upon it five little dried orange pips.

"This is the envelope", he continued. "The postmark

is London—eastern division. Within are the very words which were upon my father's last message: 'K. K. K.'; and then 'Put the papers on the sundial.'"

"What have you done?" asked Holmes.

"Nothing".

"Nothing?"

"To tell the truth"—he sank his face into his thin, white hands—"I have felt helpless. I have felt like one of those poor rabbits when the snake is writhing towards it. I seem to be in the grasp of some resistless, inexorable evil, which no foresight and no precautions can guard against".

"Tut! tut!" cried Sherlock Holmes. "You must act, man, or you are lost. Nothing but energy can save you. This is no time for despair".

"I have seen the police".

"Ah!"

"But they listened to my story with a smile. I am convinced that the inspector has formed the opinion that the letters are all practical jokes, and that the deaths of my relations were really accidents, as the jury stated, and were not to be connected with the warnings".

Holmes shook his clenched hands in the air. "Incredible imbecility!" he cried.

"They have, however, allowed me a policeman, who may remain in the house with me".

"Has he come with you tonight?"

"No. His orders were to stay in the house".

Again Holmes raved in the air.

"Why did you come to me?" he said, "and, above all, why did you not come at once?"

"I did not know. It was only today that I spoke to Major Prendergast about my troubles and was advised by him to come to you".

"It is really two days since you had the letter. We should have acted before this. You have no further evidence, I suppose, than that which you have placed before us—no suggestive detail which might help us?"

"There is one thing", said John Openshaw. He rummaged in his coat pocket, and, drawing out a piece of discoloured, blue-tinted paper, he laid it out upon the table. "I have some remembrance", said he, "that on the day when my uncle burned the papers I observed that the small, unburned margins which lay amid the ashes were of this particular colour. I found this single sheet upon the floor of his room, and I am inclined to think that it may be one of the papers which has, perhaps, fluttered out from among the others, and in that way has escaped destruction. Beyond the mention of pips, I do not see that it helps us much. I think myself that it is a page from some private diary. The writing is undoubtedly my uncle's".

Holmes moved the lamp, and we both bent over the sheet of paper, which showed by its ragged edge that it had indeed been torn from a book. It was headed, "March, 1869", and beneath were the following enigmatical notices:

"4th. Hudson came. Same old platform.

"7th. Set the pips on McCauley, Paramore, and John Swain of St. Augustine.

"9th. McCauley cleared.

"10th. John Swain cleared.

"12th. Visited Paramore. All well".

"Thank you!" said Holmes, folding up the paper and returning it to our visitor. "And now you must on no account lose another instant. We cannot spare time even to discuss what you have told me. You must get home instantly and act".

"What shall I do?"

"There is but one thing to do. It must be done at once. You must put this piece of paper which you have shown us into the brass box which you have described. You must also put in a note to say that all the other papers were burned by your uncle, and that this is the only one which remains. You must assert that in such words as will carry conviction with them. Having done this, you must at once put the box out upon the sundial, as directed. Do you understand?"

"Entirely".

"Do not think of revenge, or anything of the sort, at present. I think that we may gain that by means of the law; but we have our web to weave, while theirs is already woven. The first consideration is to remove the pressing danger which threatens you. The second is to clear up the mystery and to punish the guilty parties".

"I thank you", said the young man, rising and pulling on his overcoat. "You have given me fresh life and hope. I shall certainly do as you advise".

"Do not lose an instant. And, above all, take care of yourself in the meanwhile, for I do not think that there can be a doubt that you are threatened by a very real and imminent danger. How do you go back?"

"By train from Waterloo".

"It is not yet nine. The streets will be crowded, so I trust that you may be in safety. And yet you cannot guard yourself too closely".

"I am armed".

"That is well. To-morrow I shall set to work upon your case".

"I shall see you at Horsham, then?"

"No, your secret lies in London. It is there that I shall seek it".

"Then I shall call upon you in a day, or in two days, with news as to the box and the papers. I shall take your advice in every particular". He shook hands with us and took his leave. Outside the wind still screamed and the rain splashed and pattered against the windows. This strange, wild story seemed to have come to us from amid the mad elements—blown in upon us like a sheet of sea-weed in a gale—and now to have been reabsorbed by them once more.

Sherlock Holmes sat for some time in silence, with his head sunk forward and his eyes bent upon the red glow of the fire. Then he lit his pipe, and leaning back in his chair he watched the blue smoke-rings as they chased each other up to the ceiling.

"I think, Watson", he remarked at last, "that of all our

His eyes bent upon the glow of the fire

cases we have had none more fantastic than this".

"Save, perhaps, the Sign of Four".

"Well, yes. Save, perhaps, that. And yet this John Openshaw seems to me to be walking amid even greater perils than did the Sholtos".

"But have you", I asked, "formed any definite conception as to what these perils are?"

"There can be no question as to their nature", he answered.

"Then what are they? Who is this K. K. K., and why does he pursue this unhappy family?"

Sherlock Holmes closed his eyes and placed his elbows upon the arms of his chair, with his finger-tips together. "The ideal reasoner", he remarked, "would, when he had once been shown a single fact in all its bearings, deduce from it not only all the chain of events which led up to it but also all the results which would follow from it. As Cuvier could correctly describe a whole animal by the contemplation of a single bone, so the observer who has thoroughly understood one link in a series of incidents should be able to accurately state all the other ones, both before and after. We have not yet grasped the results which the reason alone can attain to. Problems may be solved in the study which have baffled all those who have sought a solution by the aid of their senses. To carry the art, however, to its highest pitch, it is necessary that the reasoner should be able to utilise all the facts which have come to his knowledge; and this in itself implies, as you will readily see, a possession of all knowledge, which, even in these days of free education and encyclopædias, is a somewhat rare accomplishment. It is not so impossible, however, that a man should possess all knowledge which is likely to be useful to him in his work, and this I have endeavoured in my case to do. If I remember rightly, you on one occasion, in the early days of our friendship, defined my limits in a very precise fashion".

"Yes", I answered, laughing. "It was a singular document. Philosophy, astronomy, and politics were marked at zero, I remember. Botany variable, geology profound as regards the mud-stains from any region within fifty miles of town, chemistry eccentric, anatomy unsystematic, sensational literature and crime records unique, violin-player, boxer, swordsman, lawyer, and self-poisoner by cocaine and tobacco. Those, I think, were the main points of my analysis".

Holmes grinned at the last item. "Well", he said, "I say now, as I said then, that a man should keep his little brain-attic stocked with all the furniture that he is likely to use, and the rest he can put away in the lumber-room of his library, where he can get it if he wants it. Now, for such a case as the one which has been submitted to us tonight, we need certainly to muster all our resources. Kindly hand me down the letter K of the *American Encyclopædia* which stands upon the shelf beside you. Thank you. Now let us consider the situation and see what may be deduced from it. In the first place, we may start with a strong presumption that Colonel Openshaw had some very strong reason for leaving America. Men at his time of life do not change all their habits and exchange willingly the charming climate of Florida for the lonely life of an English provincial town. His extreme love of solitude in England suggests the idea that he was in fear of someone or something, so we may assume as a working hypothesis that it was fear of someone or something which drove him from America. As to what it was he feared, we can only deduce that by considering the formidable letters which were received by himself and his successors. Did you remark the postmarks of those letters?"

"The first was from Pondicherry, the second from Dundee, and the third from London".

"From East London. What do you deduce from that?"

"They are all seaports. That the writer was on board of a ship".

"Excellent. We have already a clue. There can be no doubt that the probability—the strong probability—is that the writer was on board of a ship. And now let us consider another point. In the case of Pondicherry, seven weeks elapsed between the threat and its fulfilment, in Dundee it was only some three or four days. Does that suggest anything?"

"A greater distance to travel".

"But the letter had also a greater distance to come".

"Then I do not see the point".

"There is at least a presumption that the vessel in which the man or men are is a sailing-ship. It looks as if they always send their singular warning or token before them when starting upon their mission. You see how quickly the deed followed the sign when it came from Dundee. If they had come from Pondicherry in a steamer they would have arrived almost as soon as their letter. But, as a matter of fact, seven weeks elapsed. I think that those seven weeks represented the difference between the mail-boat which brought the letter and the sailing vessel which brought the writer".

"It is possible".

"More than that. It is probable. And now you see the deadly urgency of this new case, and why I urged young Openshaw to caution. The blow has always fallen at the end of the time which it would take the senders to travel the distance. But this one comes from London, and therefore we cannot count upon delay".

"Good God!" I cried. "What can it mean, this relentless persecution?"

"The papers which Openshaw carried are obviously of vital importance to the person or persons in the sailing-ship. I think that it is quite clear that there must be more than one of them. A single man could not have carried out two deaths in such a way as to deceive a coroner's jury. There must have been several in it, and they must have been men of resource and determination. Their papers they mean to have, be the holder of them who it may. In this way you see K. K. K. ceases to be the initials of an individual and becomes the badge of a society".

"But of what society?"

"Have you never—" said Sherlock Holmes, bending forward and sinking his voice—"have you never heard of the Ku Klux Klan?"

"I never have".

Holmes turned over the leaves of the book upon his knee. "Here it is", said he presently:

"'Ku Klux Klan. A name derived from the fanciful resemblance to the sound produced by cocking a rifle. This terrible secret society was formed by some ex-Confederate soldiers in the Southern states after the Civil War, and it rapidly formed local branches in different parts of the country, notably in Tennessee, Louisiana, the Carolinas, Georgia, and Florida. Its power was used for political purposes, principally for the terrorising of the negro voters and the murdering and driving from the country of those who were opposed to its views. Its outrages were usually preceded by a warning sent to the marked man in some fantastic but generally recognised shape—a sprig of oak-leaves in some parts, melon seeds or orange pips in others. On receiving this the victim might either openly abjure his former ways, or might fly from the country. If he braved the matter out, death would unfailingly come upon him, and usually in some strange and unforeseen manner. So perfect was the organisation of the society, and so systematic its methods, that there is hardly a case upon record where any man succeeded in braving it with impunity, or in which any of its outrages were traced home to the perpetrators. For some years the organisation flourished in spite of the efforts of the United States government and of the better classes of the community in the South. Eventually, in the year 1869, the movement rather suddenly collapsed, although there have been sporadic outbreaks of the same sort since that date.'

"You will observe", said Holmes, laying down the volume, "that the sudden breaking up of the society was coincident with the disappearance of Openshaw from America with their papers. It may well have been cause and effect. It is no wonder that he and his family have some of the more implacable spirits upon their track. You can understand that this register and diary may implicate some of the first men in the South, and that there may be many who will not sleep easy at night until it is recovered".

"Then the page we have seen—"

"Is such as we might expect. It ran, if I remember right, 'sent the pips to A, B, and C'—that is, sent the society's warning to them. Then there are successive entries that A and B cleared, or left the country, and finally that C was visited, with, I fear, a sinister result for C. Well, I think, Doctor, that we may let some light into this dark place, and I believe that the only chance young Openshaw has in the meantime is to do what I have told him. There is nothing more to be said or to be done to-night, so hand me over my violin and let us try to forget for half an hour the miserable weather and the still more miserable ways of our fellow men".

It had cleared in the morning, and the sun was shining with a subdued brightness through the dim veil which hangs over the great city. Sherlock Holmes was already at breakfast when I came down.

"You will excuse me for not waiting for you", said he; "I have, I foresee, a very busy day before me in looking into this case of young Openshaw's".

"What steps will you take?" I asked.

"It will very much depend upon the results of my first inquiries. I may have to go down to Horsham, after all".

"You will not go there first?"

"No, I shall commence with the City. Just ring the bell and the maid will bring up your coffee".

As I waited, I lifted the unopened newspaper from the table and glanced my eye over it. It rested upon a heading which sent a chill to my heart.

"Holmes", I cried, "you are too late".

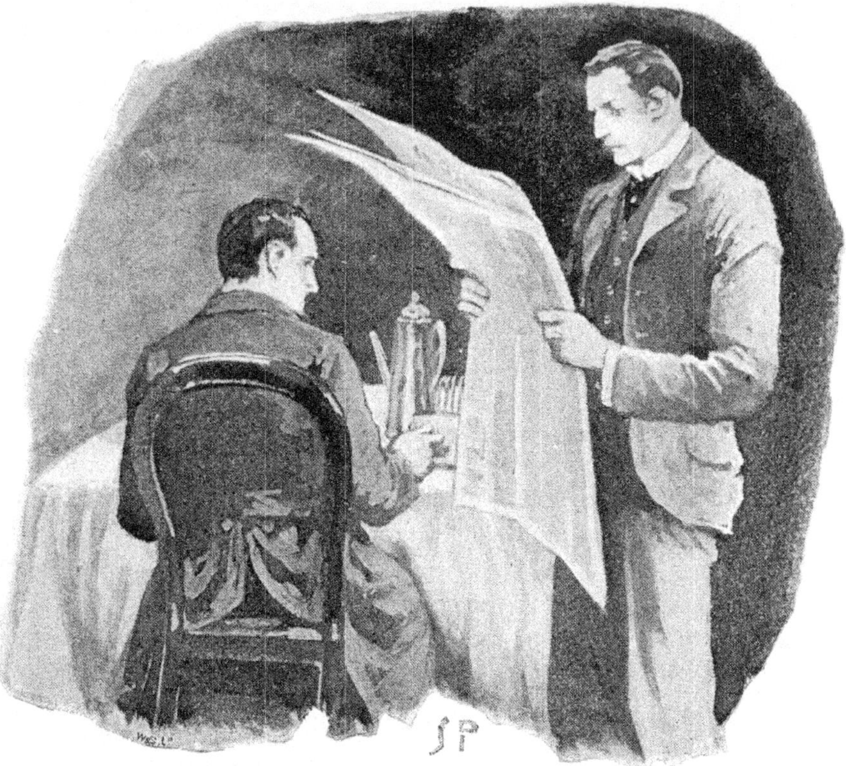

"Holmes," I cried. "You are too late."

"Ah!" said he, laying down his cup, "I feared as much. How was it done?" He spoke calmly, but I could see that he was deeply moved.

"My eye caught the name of Openshaw, and the heading 'Tragedy Near Waterloo Bridge.' Here is the account:

"'Between nine and ten last night Police-Constable Cook, of the H Division, on duty near Waterloo Bridge, heard a cry for help and a splash in the water. The night, however, was extremely dark and stormy, so that, in spite of the help of several passers-by, it was quite impossible to effect a rescue. The alarm, however, was given, and, by the aid of the water-police, the body was eventually recovered. It proved to be that of a young gentleman whose name, as it appears from an envelope which was found in his pocket, was John Openshaw, and whose residence is near Horsham. It is conjectured that he may have been hurrying down to catch the last train from Waterloo Station, and that in his haste and the extreme darkness he missed his path and walked over the edge of one of the small landing-places for river steamboats. The body exhibited no traces of violence, and there can be no doubt that the deceased had been the victim of an unfortunate accident, which should have the effect of calling the attention of the authorities to the condition of the riverside landing-stages.'"

We sat in silence for some minutes, Holmes more depressed and shaken than I had ever seen him.

"That hurts my pride, Watson", he said at last. "It is a petty feeling, no doubt, but it hurts my pride. It becomes a personal matter with me now, and, if God sends me health, I shall set my hand upon this gang. That he should come to me for help, and that I should send him away to his death—!" He sprang from his chair and paced about the room in uncontrollable agitation, with a flush upon his sallow cheeks and a nervous clasping and unclasping of his long thin hands.

"They must be cunning devils", he exclaimed at last. "How could they have decoyed him down there? The Embankment is not on the direct line to the station. The bridge, no doubt, was too crowded, even on such a night, for their purpose. Well, Watson, we shall see who will win in the long run. I am going out now!"

"To the police?"

"No; I shall be my own police. When I have spun the web they may take the flies, but not before".

All day I was engaged in my professional work, and it was late in the evening before I returned to Baker Street. Sherlock Holmes had not come back yet. It was nearly ten o'clock before he entered, looking pale and worn. He walked up to the sideboard, and tearing a piece from the loaf he devoured it voraciously, washing it down with a long draught of water.

"You are hungry", I remarked.

"Starving. It had escaped my memory. I have had nothing since breakfast".

"Nothing?"

"Not a bite. I had no time to think of it".

"And how have you succeeded?"

"Well".

"You have a clue?"

"I have them in the hollow of my hand. Young Openshaw shall not long remain unavenged. Why, Watson, let us put their own devilish trade-mark upon them. It is well thought of!"

"What do you mean?"

He took an orange from the cupboard, and tearing it to pieces he squeezed out the pips upon the table. Of these he took five and thrust them into an envelope. On the inside of the flap he wrote "S. H. for J. O". Then he sealed it and addressed it to "Captain James Calhoun, Barque Lone Star, Savannah, Georgia".

"That will await him when he enters port", said he, chuckling. "It may give him a sleepless night. He will find it as sure a precursor of his fate as Openshaw did before him".

"And who is this Captain Calhoun?"

"The leader of the gang. I shall have the others, but he first".

"How did you trace it, then?"

He took a large sheet of paper from his pocket, all covered with dates and names.

"I have spent the whole day", said he, "over Lloyd's registers and files of the old papers, following the future career of every vessel which touched at Pondicherry in January and February in '83. There were thirty-six ships of fair tonnage which were reported there during those months. Of these, one, the Lone Star, instantly attracted my attention, since, although it was reported as having cleared from London, the name is that which is given to one of the states of the Union".

"Texas, I think".

"I was not and am not sure which; but I knew that the ship must have an American origin".

"What then?"

"I searched the Dundee records, and when I found that the barque Lone Star was there in January, '85, my suspicion became a certainty. I then inquired as to the vessels which lay at present in the port of London".

"Yes?"

"The Lone Star had arrived here last week. I went down to the Albert Dock and found that she had been taken down the river by the early tide this morning, homeward bound to Savannah. I wired to Gravesend and learned that she had passed some time ago, and as the wind is easterly I have no doubt that she is now past the Goodwins and not very far from the Isle of Wight".

"What will you do, then?"

"Oh, I have my hand upon him. He and the two mates, are as I learn, the only native-born Americans in the ship. The others are Finns and Germans. I know, also, that they were all three away from the ship last night. I had it from the stevedore who has been loading their cargo. By the time that their sailing-ship reaches Savannah the mail-boat will have carried this letter, and the cable will have informed the police of Savannah that these three gentlemen are badly wanted here upon a charge of murder".

There is ever a flaw, however, in the best laid of human plans, and the murderers of John Openshaw were never to receive the orange pips which would show them that another, as cunning and as resolute as themselves, was upon their track. Very long and very severe were the equinoctial gales that year. We waited long for news of the Lone Star of Savannah, but none ever reached us. We did at last hear that somewhere far out in the Atlantic a shattered stern-post of a boat was seen swinging in the trough of a wave, with the letters "L. S". carved upon it, and that is all which we shall ever know of the fate of the Lone Star.

WHAT DID WE LEARN

The Highlights

Intricate Plot

The narrative unfolds with a mysterious series of letters containing five dried orange pips, marking the start of an unsettling puzzle.

Sinister Letters

The letters bring tragedy, with John Openshaw's uncle and father meeting untimely deaths under inexplicable circumstances.

Desperate Plea

Openshaw seeks Holmes' guidance to decipher the menacing letters and put an end to the ominous pattern of deaths.

Cryptic Threats

The recurring motif of the orange pips adds an eerie dimension to the letters' ominous message, deepening the mystery.

Holmes' Deduction

With meticulous scrutiny, Holmes unravels the letters' origin, revealing a shadowy vendetta linked to a secret society.

Unsolvable Enigma

Despite Holmes' efforts, Openshaw meets a tragic end, leaving the detective with a rare sense of helplessness and frustration.

Elusive Justice

The story challenges Holmes' pursuit of truth, underscoring the theme of unresolved terror in the face of inscrutable malevolence.

Mystery Unveiled

Through the narrative, readers experience Holmes' unwavering determination, even when faced with the unsettling and unknown.

Human Complexity

This tale delves into the intricate nature of human fear, evoking Holmes' admiration for Openshaw's courage and resilience.

Holmes' Reflection

The narrative showcases Holmes' contemplation on the limits of his deductive powers, offering a profound exploration of human vulnerability.

Lessons To Remember

The Past Can Haunt You

The events of the past, even seemingly insignificant ones, can come back to haunt you in unexpected ways.

Family Secrets

Family secrets can be dangerous, and sometimes it's necessary to confront them to prevent harm.

Fear and Paranoia

Excessive fear and paranoia can cloud judgment and lead to irrational actions.

Trust in Authorities

Trusting in the authorities, like the police or detectives, can sometimes be misplaced, and it's essential to be vigilant and seek alternative solutions.

The Power of Deduction

Holmes demonstrates the power of deductive reasoning and the importance of keen observation in solving mysteries.

Communication is Key

Poor communication can lead to misunderstandings and dire consequences, emphasizing the need for clear and effective communication.

Racism and Prejudice

The story touches on themes of racism and prejudice, highlighting the harm they can cause and the importance of tolerance and equality.

Unusual Clues:

Sometimes, the most unusual clues can hold the key to solving a mystery.

Importance of Records

Maintaining records and documentation can be crucial in solving complex problems.

The Unpredictable Nature of Life

Life is unpredictable, and even seemingly routine events can take unexpected turns, requiring adaptability and quick thinking.

Mistakes To Avoid

Ignoring Family Warnings

Don't dismiss family warnings or superstitions without careful consideration; they might contain valuable insights.

Neglecting Safety Precautions

Failing to take safety precautions in unfamiliar situations can lead to danger. Always be cautious when handling unfamiliar objects or documents.

Relying Solely on Authorities

Don't rely solely on the authorities or law enforcement to protect you.

Assuming Innocence

Avoid assuming that people are innocent solely based on their appearance or social status. Everyone should be treated with equal scrutiny until proven otherwise.

Not Investigating Thoroughly

In matters of mystery or suspicion, avoid the mistake of not investigating thoroughly. Details matter, and even seemingly insignificant clues can be vital.

Lack of Communication

Poor communication among family members can lead to misunderstandings and missed opportunities for solving problems. Keep the lines of communication open.

Prejudice and Stereotyping

Don't succumb to prejudice or stereotype people based on their backgrounds, as it can lead to incorrect judgments and missed connections.

Ignoring the Past

Neglecting to examine the past can prevent you from understanding the present. History often holds the key to solving current mysteries.

Underestimating Danger

Never underestimate the potential danger in a situation. Take threats seriously and take appropriate precautions.

Overlooking Unusual Clues

Be attentive to unusual or seemingly insignificant clues, as they may hold the answers to complex puzzles. Don't dismiss anything out of hand.

CHALLENGE
YOURSELF

Let's Get Quizzical

1. What do the mysterious letters contain?

A) Dried apricot seeds
B) Five dried orange pips
C) Black feathers
D) Tiny stones

2. Who seeks Sherlock Holmes' assistance?

A) Irene Adler
B) Dr. John Watson
C) John Openshaw
D) Wilhelm Gottsreich

3. What relationship did the recipients of the letters share?

A) Friends
B) Colleagues
C. Family members
D) Neighbors

4. Who sent the five orange pips to John Openshaw?

A) Sherlock Holmes
B) The local postman
C) The secret society
D) A childhood friend

5. What tragic events are associated with the letters?

A) Accidents
B) Robberies
C) Illnesses
D) Earthquakes

6. What is the name of the secret society mentioned in the story?

A) Kul Klux Klan
B) The Scarlet Ring
C) The Orange Order
D) The Black Brotherhood

7. Where did the Openshaw's have their estate?

A) Sussex
B) London
C) Horsham
D) Norfolk

8. How does John Openshaw's uncle die?

A) Drowning
B) Falling from a horse
C) Poisoning
D) Hanging

9. What happens to John Openshaw's uncle's papers?

A) They are buried in attic
B) They are stolen
C) They are destroyed in a fire
D) They are with the police

10. What is the significance of the five orange pips?

A) They symbolize good luck
B) They represent an invitation
C) They are a mark of death
D) They indicate secret meetings

11. What is the fate of John Openshaw's father?

A) Murdered
B) Accidentally poisoned
C) Drowned
D) Committed suicide

12. How does Holmes describe the case to Watson?

A) A straightforward robbery
B) A political conspiracy
C) An unsolvable mystery
D) A tangled web of intrigue

13. What role does Dr. John Watson play in the story?

A) He is the main antagonist
B) He is the client seeking help
C) He is Holmes' companion
D) He is a member of the secret society

14. Who is Elias Openshaw?

A) John's uncle
B) John's father
C) John's brother
D) John's cousin

15. What kind of relationship does Holmes have with the police?

A) Antagonistic
B) Distrusting
C) Amicable
D) Indifferent

16. What eventually happens to John Openshaw?

A) He is framed for a crime
B) He escapes to another country
C) He is killed by the secret society
D) His fate is left unknown

17. Who is the head of the secret society?

A) Elias Openshaw
B) John Openshaw
C) The King of Bohemia
D) It remains undisclosed

18. How does the society mark its victims?

A) With a red handprint
B) With five orange pips
C) With a black feather
D) With a coded message

19. What does Holmes advise John Openshaw to do?

A) Write a letter to KKK
B) Trust in the police
C) Stay in London
D) Flee the country immediately

20. What is the primary theme of "The Five Orange Pips"?

A) Love and romance
B) The power of wealth
C) The consequences of vengeance
D) The pursuit of fame

*Answers at the end of the book

What Do You Think?

Question 1

Why does Holmes initially underestimate the significance of the orange pips?

Clues: Consider how Holmes' focus on logic and his initial dismissal of the letters' importance may have contributed to his oversight.

Question 2

Sherlock Holmes advises John Openshaw to flee the country to escape danger. Why does Holmes recommend this course of action, and what does it reveal about his investigative approach?

Clues: Holmes's advice to John reflects his concern for his client's safety. Consider how this advice aligns with Holmes's priorities and methods.

Question 3

How do the orange pips symbolize both danger and revenge in the story?

Clues: Think about the recurring presence of the orange pips and how they connect to the victims.

*Answers at the end of the book

Complete The Crossword

Across

4. John Openshaw's uncle who received the ominous warning.

5. Dried orange symbols associated with danger.

6. Secret _______ connected to the ominous letters.

8. Motive behind the society's actions, seeking retribution.

9. Victim of the society, relative of Openshaw.

10. The secret society that sends the ominous warning.

Down

1. The five orange pips serve as this to John Openshaw.

2. Brilliant detective and protagonist of the story.

3. Ominous letters that foreshadow tragedy.

7. John _______ seeks Holmes' help regarding ominous letters.

*Answers at the end of the book

1
2
3
4
5
6
7
8
9
10

Draw and Doodle

Visualisation Exercise 1

Who do you find most captivating among the characters in this story? Illustrate any one of them in this page. Post online tagging #twagaavisuals to win exciting prices.

Visualisation Exercise 2

Which scene from this story holds a special place in your heart? Illustrate here. Post online tagging #twagaavisuals to win exciting prices.

Write Your Story

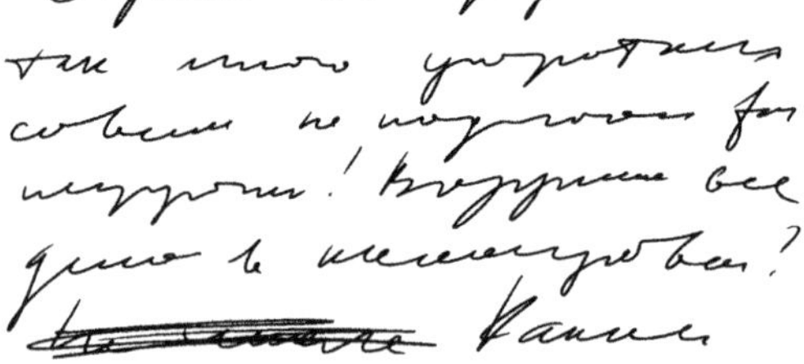

Embark on a journey of intrigue and deduction weaving secrets, disguises, and intellectual prowess to ignite your imagination and creativity to write your own detective story. Channel your inner Sherlock Holmes, to create clues, characters, and mysteries that will engage readers and challenge their minds. Follow the footsteps of Holmes and Watson, and take this opportunity to pen your own adventure, where clever deduction and unexpected twists await at every turn of the page. Step into the shoes of a master detective to create a world of suspense and enigma.

After completing your story, post it online and tag #twagaadetective to win exciting prices.

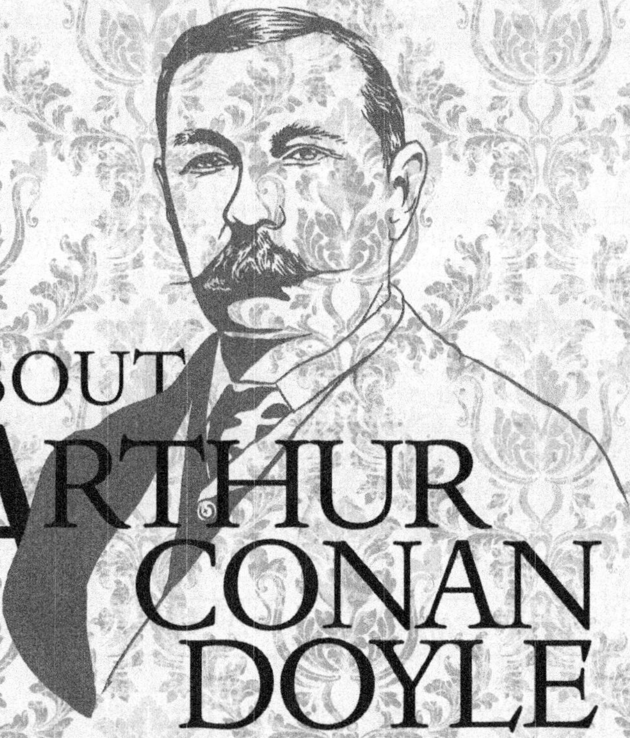

ABOUT ARTHUR CONAN DOYLE

About 'Arthur Conan Doyle'

Sir Arthur Conan Doyle (1859-1930) was a renowned Scottish writer best known for his creation of the iconic detective character, Sherlock Holmes. Born in Edinburgh, Doyle initially pursued a medical career, studying at the University of Edinburgh Medical School. However, his true passion lay in storytelling and writing.

Doyle's literary legacy is defined by his ingenious detective fiction, which revolutionized the crime genre. His first Sherlock Holmes novel, "A Study in Scarlet" (1887), introduced the world to the brilliant consulting detective Sherlock Holmes and his loyal friend Dr. John Watson. Holmes' astute reasoning, keen observation skills, and masterful deduction techniques made him an instant literary sensation.

Doyle went on to craft three more novels and 56 short stories featuring Holmes and Watson, collectively known as the "Sherlock Holmes Canon". Despite his diverse body of work, Doyle became so strongly associated with Holmes that he felt compelled to bring the detective back to life after attempting to kill him off in "The Final Problem" (1893).

Beyond Sherlock Holmes, Doyle's bibliography encompasses historical fiction, science fiction, fantasy, and non-fiction works, reflecting his multifaceted talents and wide-ranging interests. His impact on popular culture is immeasurable, as Sherlock Holmes continues to captivate audiences through adaptations, pastiches, and new interpretations, ensuring that Conan Doyle's literary legacy endures as a cornerstone of detective fiction.

About 'Sidney Edward Paget'

Sidney Edward Paget (1860-1908) is renowned for crafting the iconic image of Sherlock Holmes, deeply ingrained in popular culture. His illustrations, published alongside Arthur Conan Doyle's detective stories in the Strand Magazine from 1891, became inseparable from the Sherlock Holmes canon. Even Conan Doyle admitted Paget's portrayal surpassed his own written description of the Great Detective.

Born in London in 1860, Paget received his education at various institutions before delving into art. He won recognition at the Royal Academy Schools and pursued portraiture and magazine illustrations, earning fame for his meticulous work. In 1893, he married Edith Hounsfield and had six children. Despite his success, Paget battled health issues, possibly due to lead-based paint ingestion from brushes. He passed away in 1908.

Paget's impact as a Sherlock Holmes illustrator remains indelible, as he produced over 350 black-and-white drawings for the stories, greatly contributing to their popularity. He added distinct features to Holmes's image, such as the deerstalker hat and Inverness cape, even though Conan Doyle never explicitly described these details. These elements have become synonymous with Holmes's character. Paget's work solidified the enduring visual representation of Holmes, influencing subsequent illustrators. In recognition of his contribution, Conan Doyle gifted Paget a silver cigarette case inscribed "From Sherlock Holmes, 1893." Though most of his original drawings have been lost, his legacy endures through the surviving illustrations that continue to captivate enthusiasts and collectors.

Answers

Let's Get Quizzical

1. B	2. C	3. C	4. B	5. A	6. A	7. A	8. B
9. C	10. C	11. A	12. D	13. C	14. A	15. C	16. C
17. D	18. B	19. D	20. C				

What Do You Think?

Answer 1: Holmes, known for his deductive reasoning, initially dismisses the orange pips as a trivial matter due to his logical approach. He fails to grasp the broader threat they symbolize, highlighting the limitations of solely relying on logic and underestimating the potential dangers.

Answer 2: Holmes recommends John's flight to ensure his safety because he understands the seriousness of the threat posed by the Ku Klux Klan. This reveals Holmes's commitment to protecting his clients from harm, even if it means delaying the resolution of the mystery, showing his pragmatic and protective approach to investigations.

Answer 3: The orange pips represent danger and revenge as they foretell tragedy, symbolizing a malevolent force seeking vengeance against recipients. They serve as ominous warnings and mark individuals for harm, embodying both the threat and the intent of revenge that haunts the story's victims.

Complete the Crossword

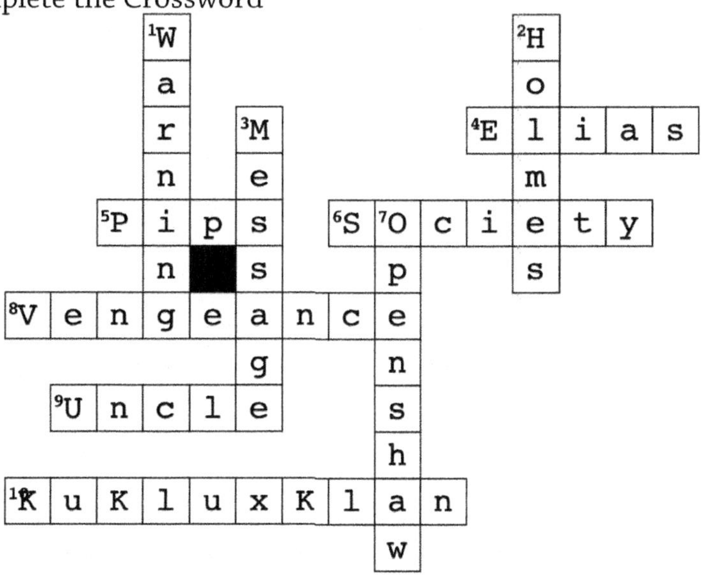

Collect Them All

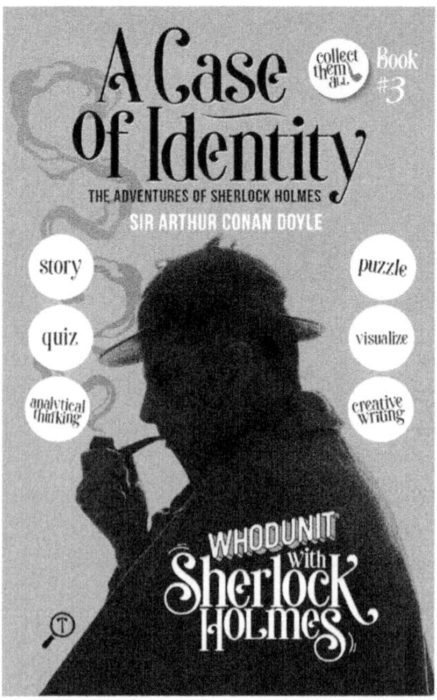

Collect Them All

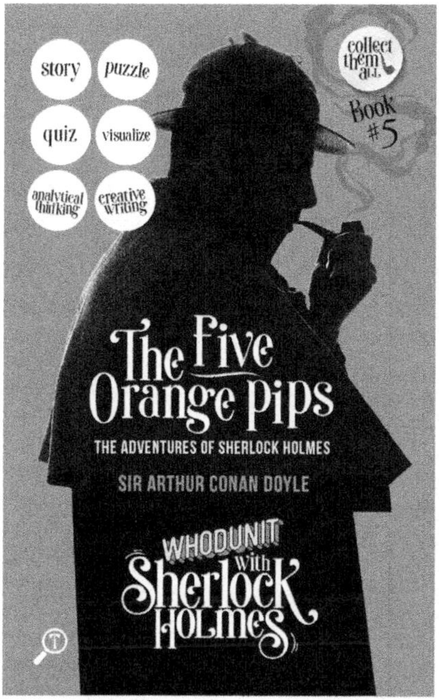

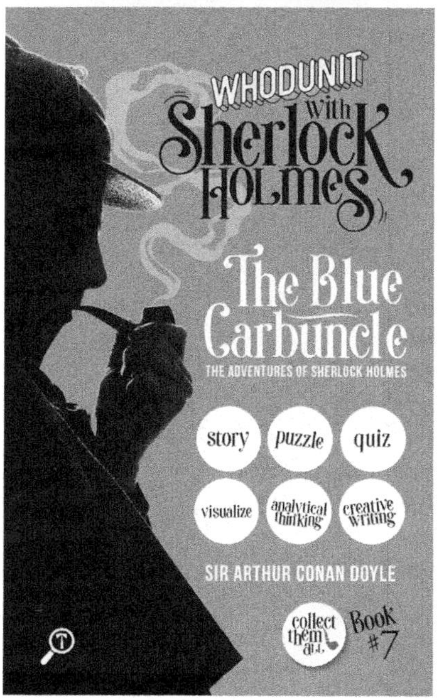

Collect Them All

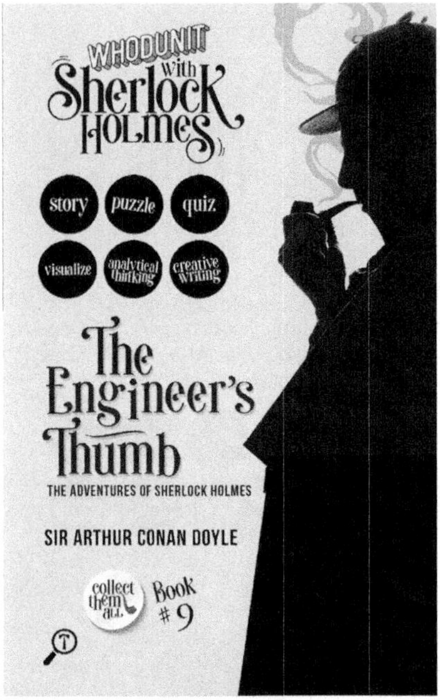

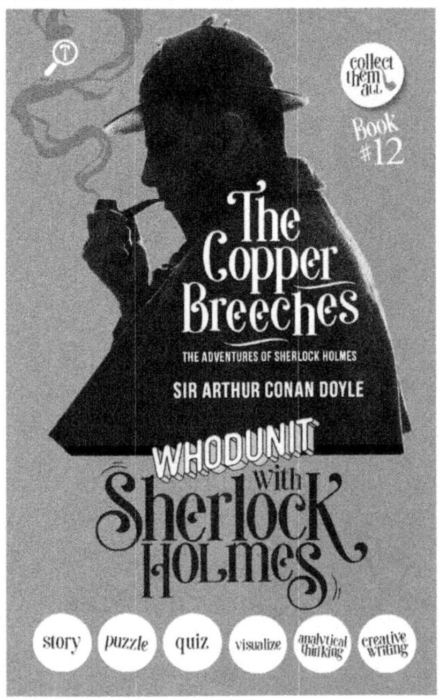

Collect Them All

*Coming Soon

The Memoirs of Sherlock Holmes

Silver Blaze
The Cardboard Box
The Yellow Face
The Stockbroker's Clerk
The Gloria Scott
The Musgrave Ritual
The Reigate Squire
The Crooked Man
The Resident Patient
The Greek Interpreter
The Naval Treaty
The Final Problem

The Return of Sherlock Holmes

The Empty House
The Norwood Builder
The Dancing Men
The Solitary Cyclist
The Priory School
The Black Peter
Charles Augustus Milverton
The Six Napoleons
The Three Students
The Golden Pince-Nez
The Missing Three-Quarter
The Abbey Grange
The Second Stain

His Last Bow

The Wisteria Lodge
The Bruce-Partington Plans
The Devil's Foot
The Red Circle
The Disappearance of Lady Frances Carfax
The Dying Detective
His Last Bow

The Case-Book of Sherlock Holmes

The Mazarin Stone
The Problem of Thor Bridge
The Creeping Man
The Sussex Vampire
The Three Garridebs
The Illustrious Client
The Three Gables
The Blanched Soldier
The Lion's Mane
The Retired Colourman
The Veiled Lodger
Shoscombe Old Place

Collect Them All

*Coming Soon

Novel

A Study In Scarlet
The Sign Of The Four
The Hound Of Baskervilles
The Valley Of Fear

Editor's Choice (The 12 best stories)

1. The Speckled Band
2. The Red-Headed League
3. The Dancing Men
4. The Final Problem
5. A Scandal in Bohemia
6. The Empty House
7. The Five Orange Pips
8. The Second Stain
9. The Devil's Foot
10. The Priory School
11. The Musgrave Ritual
12. The Reigate Squires

Collection (Set of books)

The Adventures (12 books)
The Memoirs (12 books)
The Return (13 books)
His Last Bow (7 books)
The Case-Book (12 books)

Compilations in 1 book

The Adventures (12 stories)
The Memoirs (12 stories)
The Return (13 stories)
His Last Bow (7 stories)
The Case-Book (13 stories)
Novels (4 novels)
The Complete Sherlock Holmes (58 stories + 4 novels)

Dressed like a common loafer
(The Beryl Coronet)

Carefully tear this page and frame the art

Then he stood before the fire
(A Scandal In Bohemia)

Carefully tear this page and frame the art

All afternoon he sat in the stalls
(The Red-Headed League)

For a long time he remained there (The Boscombe Valley Mystery)

Carefully tear this page and frame the art

His eyes bent upon the glow of the fire
(The Five Orange Pips)

Carefully tear this page and frame the art

The pipe was still between his lips
(The Man With The Twisted Lip)

TWAGAA

Together We Are Great, Amazing & Awesome

Countless brilliant concepts are often lost within the confines of our minds, notebooks, and hard drives. We possess the vision, but uncertainties shroud our ability to bring these visions to fruition.

At TWAGAA, we nurture the seeds of creativity within individuals, watching them flourish and thrive. We empower creative minds to unleash their full potential, guiding them on a transformative journey that brings their ideas to life in captivating and meaningful ways.

Our mission is to inspire and support the dreams of both individual and collective creative minds, harmonizing their efforts with the proven best practices of the industry.

Our offerings encompass a diverse range of products, including books, art prints, apparels, merchandises, and games. Each creation is a testament to the limitless potential of human creativity, and we're here to make sure those potentials are realized.

Know more about us at https://twagaa.com/

Printed in Great Britain
by Amazon

60117172R00058